What's the Time, MR WOLF?

For Frances, Jock and Emily Connolly.
Happy reading ~ C. J.

First American edition 1999
Originally published in Australia by HarperCollins*Publishers* Pty Limited
as an Angus&Robertson book

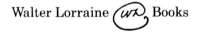

Walter Lorraine Books

Library of Congress Cataloguing-in-Publication Data:
Jones, Carol.
What's the time, Mr. Wolf? / Carol Jones.—1st American ed.
p.   cm.
Summary: In this story based on a school-yard game, the farmyard animals ask Mr. Wolf what
time it is, while he tries to lure them to come that evening to a very
special meal. At various points, a peep-hole allows a glimpse of the next illustration.

ISBN 0–395–95800–8.
1. Toy and movable books--Specimens.
[1. Wolves--Fiction. 2. Domestic animals--Fiction. 3. Time--Fiction.
4. Clocks and watches--Fiction. 5. Toy and movable books.] I. Title.
PZ7.J68157Wh   1999
[E]--dc21   98-29211
CIP
AC
For information about this and other Houghton Mifflin trade
and reference books and multimedia products, visit The Bookstore
at Houghton Mifflin on the World Wide Web at
http://www.hmco.com/trade/.

Printed in Hong Kong.

10 9 8 7 6 5 4 3 2 1

What's the Time, MR WOLF?

CAROL JONES

Houghton Mifflin Company Boston 1999

Walter Lorraine Books

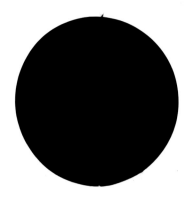

'It's . . . EIGHT O'CLOCK!'

answered Mr Wolf. 'Time for breakfast.'

Mr Wolf climbed out of bed, stretched his lean hungry body
and fixed his cold grey eyes on the plump body of his visitor.

'Rooster,' he requested, 'could you and your friends
go to the library to borrow me some new
cookery books?' He licked his lips.
'I'm planning a VERY special meal tonight!'

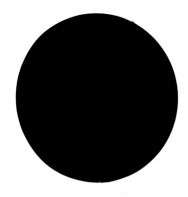

'It's . . . TEN O'CLOCK!'

answered Mr Wolf. 'Time to go shopping.'

Mr Wolf leaned on his garden fork and fixed his cold grey eyes
on the firm flanks of his visitor.

'Goat,' he asked, 'while I finish digging up the new potatoes
would you and your friends take this shopping
list to the corner shop?' He licked his lips.
'Don't forget the large bottle of tomato sauce.
I'm planning a VERY special meal tonight!'

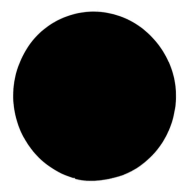

'It's ... TWELVE O'CLOCK!'

answered Mr Wolf. 'Time to go swimming.'

Mr Wolf put down his cookery book and fixed his cold grey eyes
on the chubby legs of his visitor.

'Sheep,' he said, 'go with your friends to the beach
and enjoy yourselves.' He licked his lips.
'Could you buy a bottle of mint sauce on the way?
I'm planning a VERY special meal tonight!'

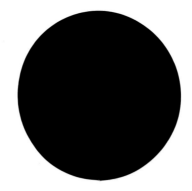

'It's . . . TWO O'CLOCK!'

answered Mr Wolf. 'Time to play.'

Mr Wolf held his wooden spoon and fixed his cold grey eyes
on the round rump of his visitor.

'Cow,' he wheedled, 'would you and your friends go into the
garden and play?' He licked his lips.
'But first can you go out and buy me a jar of hot mustard sauce?
I'm planning a VERY special meal tonight!'

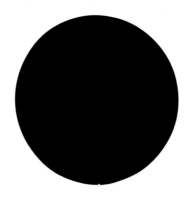

'It's . . . FOUR O'CLOCK!'

answered Mr Wolf. 'Time to get ready.'

Mr Wolf placed the salt and pepper shakers on the dining table
and turned his cold grey eyes on the portly pink figure of his visitor.

'Pig,' he insisted, 'go with your friends to the
bathroom to wash yourselves.' He licked his lips.
'But first can you go out and buy me a bottle of apple sauce?
I'm planning a VERY special meal tonight!'

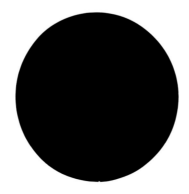

'It's . . . SIX O'CLOCK!'

answered Mr Wolf. 'Time to begin the party.'

Mr Wolf straightened his tie and turned his cold grey eyes
on the smooth white-feathered chest of his visitor.

'Duck,' he asked, 'would you and your friends like
to put on your party hats?' He licked his lips.
'But first could you pick me some oranges?
I'm planning a VERY special meal tonight!'

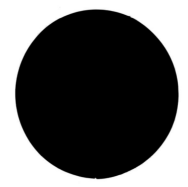

'It's . . . DINNER TIME!'

answered Mr Wolf.

'But no need to get anything, Turkey,' he said.
'I **HAVE** the cranberry sauce!'